PIPPA GOODHART ~ PHILIP HURST

FIRE CAT

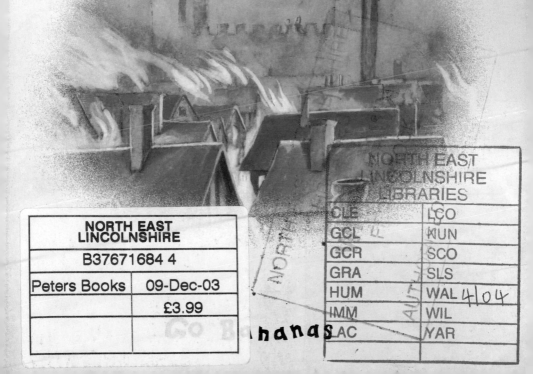

hanas

For John Robinson

P.G.

For James Hurst

P.H.

First published in Great Britain 2002
by Egmont Books Ltd
239 Kensington High Street, London W8 6SA
Text copyright © Pippa Goodhart 2002
Illustrations copyright © Philip Hurst 2002
The author and illustrator have asserted their moral rights
Photograph of extract from Pepys' Diary © copyright Magdalen College, Cambridge
Paperback ISBN 1 4052 0130 4
10 9 8 7 6 5 4 3 2 1
A CIP catalogue record for this title is available from the British Library
Printed in U.A.E.

John's Diary
1666

Sunday, 2nd September

Today has been very strange. Loud voices woke me early, so I hurried to find Father to see what the matter was.

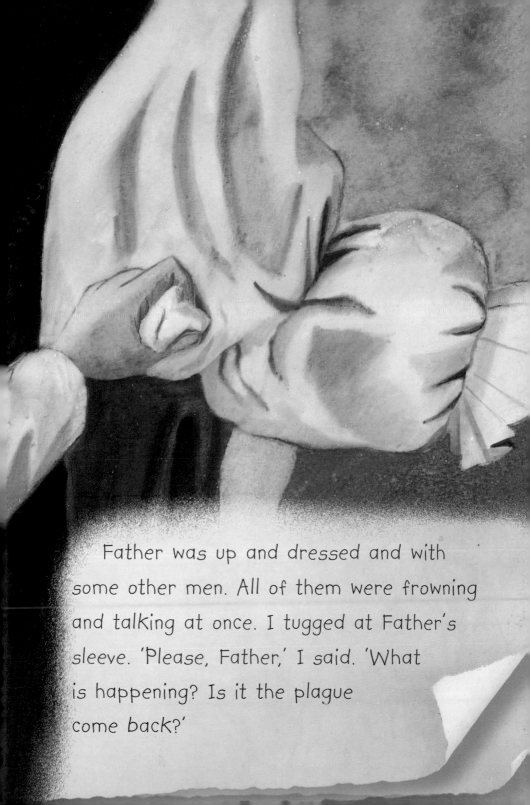

Father was up and dressed and with some other men. All of them were frowning and talking at once. I tugged at Father's sleeve. 'Please, Father,' I said. 'What is happening? Is it the plague come back?'

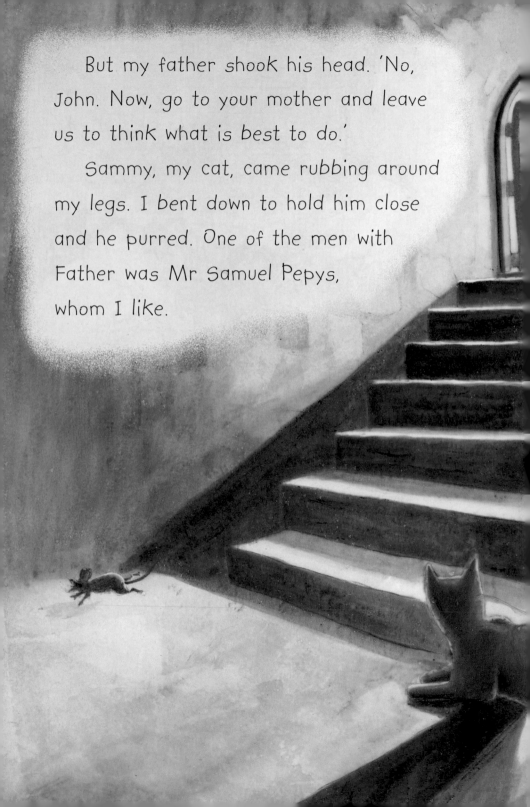

But my father shook his head. 'No, John. Now, go to your mother and leave us to think what is best to do.'

Sammy, my cat, came rubbing around my legs. I bent down to hold him close and he purred. One of the men with Father was Mr Samuel Pepys, whom I like.

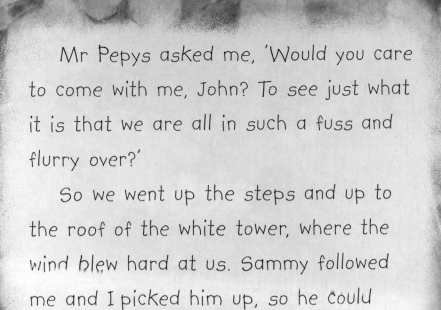

Mr Pepys asked me, 'Would you care to come with me, John? To see just what it is that we are all in such a fuss and flurry over?'

So we went up the steps and up to the roof of the white tower, where the wind blew hard at us. Sammy followed me and I picked him up, so he could see too as we looked down on London.

'Look at that,' said Mr Pepys. 'What a
sight. What a tragedy.'

London is on fire. All around the streets
are burning with bright flames and black smoke.

'Three hundred homes are already burnt,'
Mr Pepys said. 'And this gusty wind is like
a great bellows fanning the fire.'

'Will the tower burn, Mr Pepys?' I asked.
The Tower of London is my home because
my father is in charge of it. But the tower
belongs to the king. It has his jewels and
guns and all sorts stored safe inside.

'I think the tower will stay safe,' said Mr Pepys. 'It is made of stone and has the moat of water all around it.'

I thought then of how the houses along the streets in the city are nearly all made of wood. They are very close together. We have had baking-hot weather for weeks and everything is as dry as firewood.

We watched flames curling and
jumping from house to house,
pouncing like a cat after a mouse.
'The fire is like Sammy when
he is hunting,' I said.

'Like some great fire cat,' agreed Mr Pepys, and he ran a finger over Sammy's head. 'I am afraid that there is plenty for a fire cat to feed upon in our city. Think of all the oil and brandy and tar in the warehouses along the river.'

'Is there nothing that can stop the fire?' I asked.

'Only the river,' said Mr Pepys.
'Fire cannot burn water.'

'Or earth,' I said. 'They should take
away some houses or the fire will go
on and on and swallow all
of London.'

Mr Pepys looked at me then.
'My goodness, boy, you are quite right.
I must go!'

He raced down the steps. I could
hardly keep up because Sammy is
a big fat cat to carry.

'Where are you going? I asked.

'I am going to see the king,' he said. 'I shall tell his Majesty that he must order his men to pull down some houses so that the fire starves and dies before it destroys the whole city.'

Then Mr Pepys stopped still and looked at me. 'Today is a day like no other, John. You should write it down.'

'Write what down, sir?' I asked.

Mr Pepys waved a hand. 'All of it,' he said. 'Write a journal as I do every day, then you will remember it all.'

'I will,' I told him. 'And I will put you in my journal, Mr Pepys.'

'Then I shall mention you in my journal too,' smiled Mr Pepys.

So I found this book and have begun my journal. Mr Pepys said that I should put the date so that I will remember the exact day.

Ink has splattered on my new book because Sammy jumped up and pushed his face at the quill as I wrote. He wanted me to feed him, but I pushed him away and shut him out of my room. He doesn't understand that my writing is important.

Monday, 3rd September

Sammy has disappeared!
I cannot find him anywhere.
Many of our friends are
bringing their goods here
to be kept safe, in case
the fire burns their homes.
The servants have been
busy carrying in boxes
and barrels and chairs
and chests and all
sorts. I wondered if
that had frightened
Sammy.

I searched all morning in the places where I know that Sammy likes to go. I asked Mother if the servants could help me look for him, but she said, 'Can you not see that they and we are too busy to worry over cats?' She had an arm around a lady friend of hers whose house is burning at this moment.

'Please,' I asked the lady. 'Did you *see* a cat the colour of gingerbread on your way here?'

'Go away, John!' said my mother.

So I went outside, into the hot wind and the smell of fire. I leaned against the strong cool tower wall and put my hands over my ears. This is my best way to think.

Father told me that
the fire started from
a spark in a bakery in
Pudding Lane. I know
that bakery. It has
smells of warm bread.
Sammy likes the smell
of the fish stalls better.
Fish Street! What if
Sammy has gone there
looking for fish heads?
Somehow, tomorrow,
I must go and see.

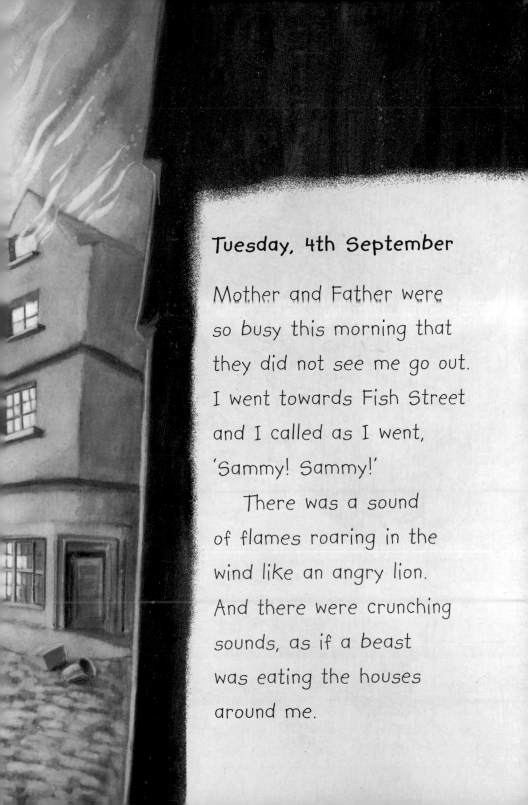

Tuesday, 4th September

Mother and Father were
so busy this morning that
they did not see me go out.
I went towards Fish Street
and I called as I went,
'Sammy! Sammy!'

There was a sound
of flames roaring in the
wind like an angry lion.
And there were crunching
sounds, as if a beast
was eating the houses
around me.

As I got close, the flames so scorched my eyes that I had to cover them with my hands. I felt like a bit of meat roasting on a spit.

'Sammy!' I shouted, but the smoke made me cough and Sammy did not come. The streets were full of people of all kinds hurrying from the fire. They were carrying whatever they could rescue from their homes.

I saw Jenny who used to serve at our table. She was carrying her baby and both of them were crying. Jenny shouted over to me, 'Go back home, Master John! There's nothing but danger here!' She was right. I don't think Sammy would stay in a place like that, unless he was trapped. Oh, I hope that he is not!

Nothing is left of Fish Street. The
stalls of silvery fish are quite gone. Every
house is burned down and all colour gone
from the place. All that is left are piles
of burned brick and black and white ash.
Smoke billows from them and sparks blow
on the wind. Nothing is alive there any more.

It was too hot and horrible. I ran home. Mother saw me coming through the door.

'John, you're filthy!' she said. 'Go and wash at once. We are about to eat.'

'Has Sammy been found?' I asked.

'I think not,' she said. Then she hurried off to see to the guests.

Wednesday, 5th September

Last night, my father and some others were going on to the river to see how the fire goes.

'May I come too?' I asked. 'Please? Mr Pepys told me that I should record it all. If I go with you then I will see more to write about. And maybe . . .'

'You just might find Sammy?' said
Father. 'You may come, John, but
you are not to get in the way.'
We took a boat under London
Bridge to see where the fire was
burning most fiercely. Even on the
water and with the sun gone down
the air was very hot from the
fire. My eyes burned so that
I could hardly keep them
open to look.

The river was like a mirror so that it seemed as if the Thames burned too, beautiful and terrifying. A full moon shone silver over the golden fire. I told my father, 'The fire is the same colour as Sammy.'

The smoky air made me choke, so I held my sleeve across my face and breathed through that, and listened to my father and his friends talking of big things.

'St. Paul's Cathedral is made of stone
and should surely stand firm,' said one.

'But so many houses lost!' said another.
'Thousands of people camp in the fields,
but whatever will they do in the weeks
ahead with winter on its way?'

Then I saw something and I stood up, rocking the boat. 'Look, Father!' I said. 'There's Sammy!'

There were boats of all kinds around us, many of them loaded with people and things. But I saw something move on one boat. It could have been a cat and I'm sure that it was a golden colour.

'Do you *see*, Father?' I asked.

'Sit down, John!' said my father. 'If that is a cat, then it is a cat that belongs to the people it is with.'

We rowed on, but I kept looking at that boat. I thought that maybe somebody had stolen Sammy. He is such a very beautiful cat.

Soon my father made the boatman
turn our boat for home. The boat with
the cat rowed on up the river and away.
I am sure that the cat was watching me.

'Go to the house, John,' said my
father when we landed. 'I have
things to see to.'

Father walked away.
But I had to find that
boat, in case it was
Sammy I had seen.

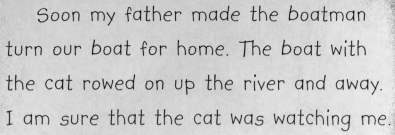

I hid until Father was out of sight and our boatman had gone for a drink. Then I ran low like a cat and I dropped back into our boat. I undid the rope and pushed away from the bank with an oar.

If our boatman was shouting after me,
I couldn't hear above all the other noise of
the firey night. I put the oars in place and
pulled as hard as I could, out into the river.
I have often watched boatmen, but rowing
is not as easy as it looks. The water soon
snatched an oar from me and I was left
with only one.

When I pulled on that oar, it took the boat round in circles, and all the time Sammy was going further away, and more boats were on the river and people shouting.

Then a great explosion crashed the air all around and fire rained on to the water. I let go of my other oar then. I went down on my knees and prayed to God as sparks fell all around. A warehouse full of tar had exploded in the heat. The tide pulled my boat under the bridge and away. I saw the king and his brother in their grand golden barge. Then I saw a boat with Mr Pepys in it.

Mr Pepys called across to me, 'Whatever are you doing in a boat alone, John?'

'Looking for my cat, sir,' I told him. The smoke from the fire made my voice choke and I could say no more as Mr Pepys came near.

'Your parents will be frightened for you, just as you are frightened for your Sammy,' said Mr Pepys. 'We must get you safely home.'

Mr Pepys took me into his boat and my boat was towed behind. I cried then, thinking of Sammy and my mother and the fire.

'There now,' said Mr Pepys. 'This fire makes us all do strange things. I myself have dug holes in my garden in middle of the night.

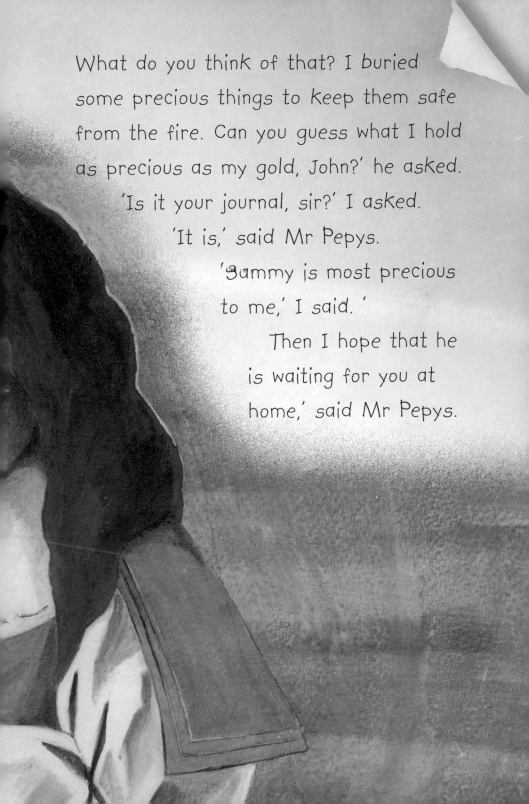

What do you think of that? I buried
some precious things to keep them safe
from the fire. Can you guess what I hold
as precious as my gold, John?' he asked.
'Is it your journal, sir?' I asked.
'It is,' said Mr Pepys.
'Gammy is most precious
to me,' I said. '
Then I hope that he
is waiting for you at
home,' said Mr Pepys.

But he wasn't. My mother took hold
of me when I got home. 'Wherever
have you been, John?'

'Looking for Sammy,' I said.

But she was too busy
to listen. 'We have guests
and you must give up
your bed and sleep on
the floor tonight, John.
Take the sheets from
your room and bring
them down here.'

I went slowly up the stairs.
I smelt of sweat and smoke
and I wanted Sammy so much
that I hurt inside.

In my room I took hold
of a handful of sheet to wipe
my face. Then, 'Meow', I
heard. And I knew then and
I laughed out loud. 'Sammy!'

I lifted the cover and saw
Sammy snug on my bed. In
the curl of his tummy were
three tiny kittens. 'Sammy,
you clever boy!'

Mother came into my
room behind me.

'Look!' I said. 'Sammy's got three kittens!'
Mother put an arm around me. 'Then I
think that your Sammy must be a 'she' and
not a 'he', don't you?'

But I didn't mind. I stroked the kittens
very gently with one finger, and Mother did
too. They were warm and damp and
had their eyes tightly closed.

They made little noises. Sammy purred.
I asked Mother, 'When the fire is over, do
you think that Mr Pepys would like it if I
gave him one of the kittens?'

'I think that he might,' said my mother.

I think so too. I think that I would like
to give him the handsomest one of all.

We will make new building rules.

We must rebuild our buildings from stone and brick to make them safe.

NOBODY wanted such a fire to start again, so they thought hard about how to prevent it.

So the fire wasn't all bad then!

JUST before the Great Fire of London, many thousands of people had died from a terrible disease called 'the Plague', which was carried by rats. The Great Fire of London destroyed the areas where most of the rats lived.

YEAR

1633 — 1660 — 1660 — 1665 — 1666 —

23rd February Pepys' birth

Pepys started writing his diary

Coronation of King Charles II

The Plague began

The Great Fire of London

S AMUEL Pepys wrote a diary that became very famous. People all over the world still enjoy reading it! Pepys' diary tells us a lot about the important things that happened during his lifetime, like the Plague and the Great Fire of London. But Pepys also wrote about his friends and family and about things that he saw and enjoyed. Pepys was very fond of food and often describes what he had for dinner!

January 26th, 1659:
'. . . a dish of marrow bones, a leg of mutton; a loin of veal; a dish of fowl; three pullets, and two dozen larks, all in a great dish!'

P EPYS' diary is great fun! When we read it we can really imagine what it was like to live in the seventeenth century.

1669

Pepys stopped
writing his diary

1703
26th May
Pepys' death

1825
Pepys' diary made
into a book

2000

The Great Fire of
London happened
over three hundred
years ago.

Why don't you write a diary like Pepys?

Maybe in the future someone will read your diary, and it will help them to understand what your life was like. It will be fascinating to them, just as Pepys' diary is fascinating to us!

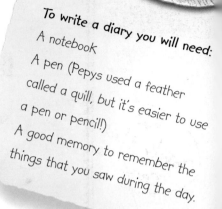

To write a diary you will need:

A notebook

A pen (Pepys used a feather called a quill, but it's easier to use a pen or pencil!)

A good memory to remember the things that you saw during the day.

Pepys didn't want people to read some of the things he wrote in his diary, so he wrote in code! The picture below is an extract from Pepys' diary.

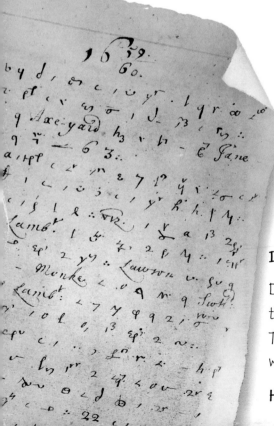

If you want to write secrets in your diary, why don't you try using a code too! Try putting the first letter of each word last like this:

Hist si ym ecrets iaryd - Eepk Uto!

This is my secret diary - Keep Out!

It will take a detective to crack it!

Don't forget to write the date at the top, just like John did in the story! Then you'll remember which day you were writing about.

Have fun writing your diary!